Chelsea's Healthy Secrets

written by
Dr. Sherry Schiavi
illustrated by
Elizabeth Huffmaster

We want to hear from you. Please send your comments about this book to us
in care of the address below. Thank you.

CELLTRITION™

Chelsea's Healthy Secrets™
Copyright © 2003 by Sherry Schiavi
First Edition, 2003
2nd Edition, 2008

Illustrated by Elizabeth Huffmaster
Edited by Joyce Svoboda Bordlee, Dr. Winston A. Churchill Lewis, Monique F. Dees

Book and Cover designed by Deziner Media International

Requests for information should be addressed to:
CELLTRITION™
Living Waters Medical Center
13472 Vidalia Road
Pass Christian, MS 39571
www.chelseashealthysecrets.com

ISBN: 0-9746378-0-7
Library of Congress Control Number: 2004100448

Printed in the U.S.A.

Special thanks to my husband *Dr. Frank Schiavi, Jr.* and to my mother *Joyce Svoboda Bordlee.*

This book is dedicated to all children everywhere, who will live healthier and happier lives because of learning Chelsea's Healthy Secrets.

CELLTRITION

Hi! My name is Chelsea.

Friends call me Healthy Chelsea

because from sickness I am free.

It's fun to be so healthy

with lots of energy!

The reason I'm so healthy
is because of what I put inside of me.

I feel so very sorry for my good friend Rick.
He is often tired,
and misses school because he is sick.

I think I'll visit Rick,

and check on him today.

Maybe this time he will be able

to come outside and play.

"Hi Rick! Can you come
outside with me and play?"
"No Chelsea, I wish I could...
but I'm feeling sick today."

I'll sit on the sofa

and have chips and soda pop.

Maybe my headache will go away.

Perhaps it will stop.

I'm so-o-o very sorry Rick

to find you're feeling tired and sick.

Remember, tomorrow our school

is having a big HEALTH FAIR.

I really do hope that you will be there.

Rick and Chelsea

go to the health fair at school.

Good morning class! I'm your health teacher.
My name is Mrs. Nell.
Today you will learn SECRETS
about being healthy and staying well.
Listen closely everyone,
and we will all have lots of fun!

13

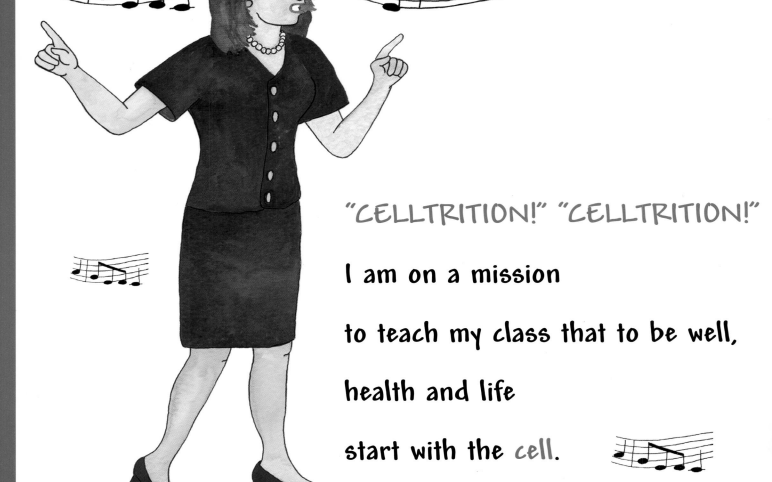

"CELLTRITION!" "CELLTRITION!"

I am on a mission

to teach my class that to be well,

health and life

start with the cell.

"What is a cell?"

Cells are what we're made of.
They are the smallest part
of all our organs, bones and muscles
and even our brain and heart.

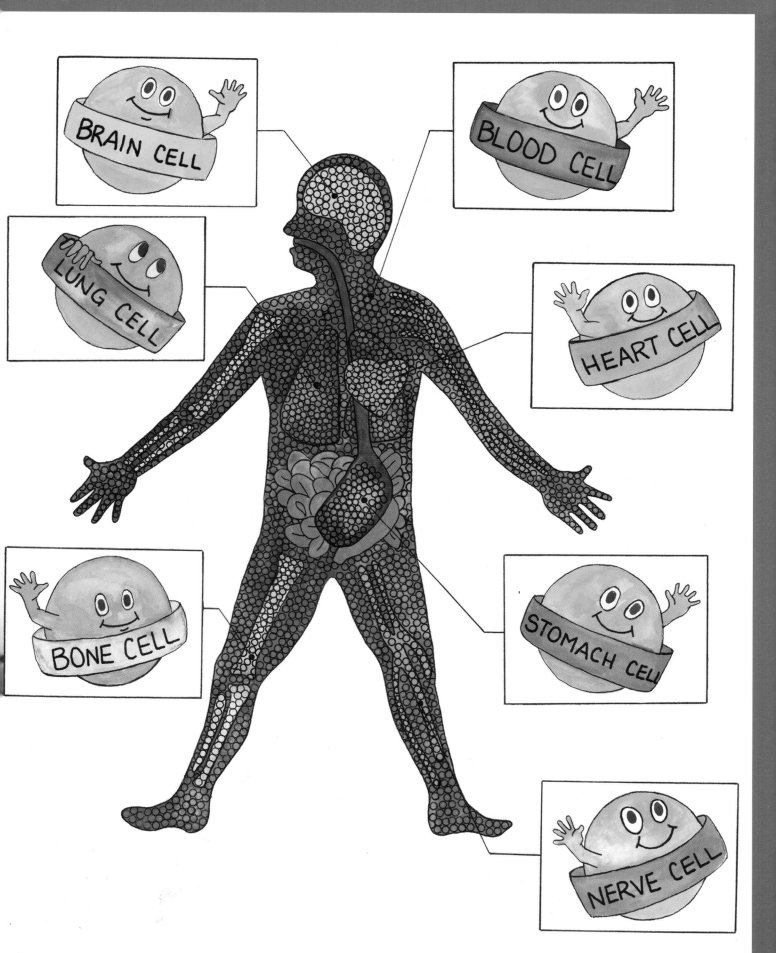

Our bodies are made up of each cell,

designed to be strong and well.

Because of unhealthy habits that we have formed,

our cells are often damaged and harmed.

Now you'll learn how to choose what is healthy and right,

so that many diseases you won't have to fight.

Your body is like a factory

that turns the food you eat into new cells and energy.

So you see, it is what we eat

that makes our cells healthy and complete.

Some foods are good for our cells
and some are bad.
Some make them happy,

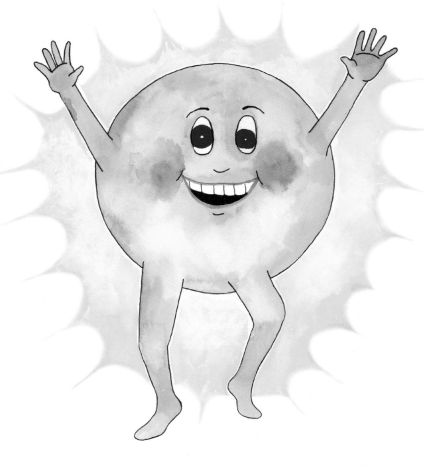

and some make them sad.

Now children, lend me your ear,

and wonderful healthy cell secrets

you will hear.

Secret 1:

Because our cells are many, and because they are alive, they need lots of good clean water, and LIVING raw fruits and veggies on which to thrive.

"Life Comes From Life"

Vitamins and minerals too,
are all needed inside of you.
Now, I'll tell you where they are found;
in fresh fruits and vegetables they abound.

23

Fun Activity

Take a raw carrot and cut the bottom off, so that the stump is about 1 inch in length. Put the carrot stump in a small container and add about a 1/2 inch of water--enough to go halfway up the carrot. Place the container in an area where it receives light. As the water disappears, replace it.

Next, freeze a second carrot and cook a third carrot (microwave, bake, steam, etc). As with the raw carrot, cut their bottoms off and place each carrot into

Life lives in Raw Food

separate, but similiar containers. Add the same amount of water as you did with the raw carrot. Place the dishes next to the raw carrot. Watch and see what happens.

If done properly, in about two weeks, you will see a plant with green leaves grow out of the raw carrot, while the cooked and frozen carrots will decay.

This demonstrates the concept that
life comes from life.

Secret 2: "Cells Need Water"

A big part of our cells is water,

and they lose lots of water each day.

To keep them from shriveling up like raisins;

DRINK WATER!

Another reason cells cry for water

is because they need it to stay clean;

like dirty clothes

in a washing machine.

Secret 3: "Sugar Blues"

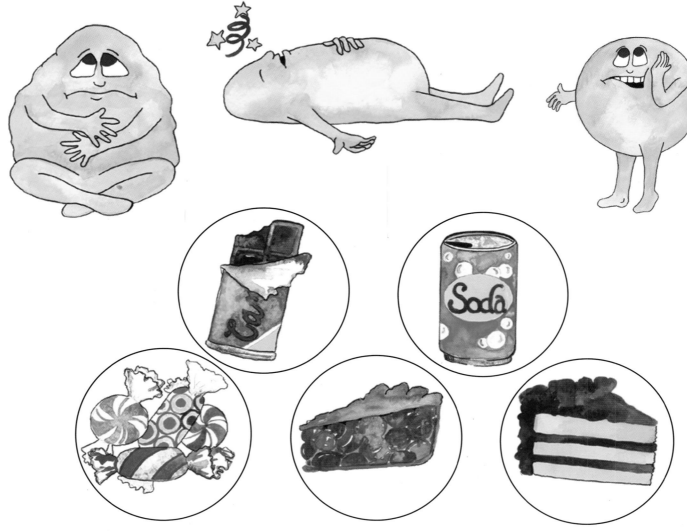

Too much sugar harms and destroys.
It robs health from girls and boys.
Sweets can cause tooth decay
when you eat them everyday.
Sugar can be addicting,
and make you always want more.
Be smart;
buy healthy snacks at the store.

Seeds and nuts are not only for birds and squirrels.
They make great snacks for boys and girls.

Secret 4:

Muscle cells increase in strength, health, and size
when we get lots of exercise.

Exercise is physical activity,
and it is much healthier than watching TV.

"Cells Need Exercise"

Breathe deeply, run, jump, and play;
and you'll enjoy your exercise each day.

Secret 5:  SOUNDS

Words are made of sounds.
Sounds are made of waves.
Listen children,
I'll show you how it behaves...

Words that are unkind,
cruel, or mean,
hurt us on the inside where
it can't be seen.

Words that are
friendly and kind
are good for our
body, soul, and mind.

Fun Activity:
Friendly Words

In this experiment, each person pairs up with another person. No unkind or unfriendly words may be spoken. Both individuals must speak 3 kind comments to the other person.

Some examples:

"I like you."
"You are fun to be with."
"I'm glad we are friends."
"You are nice."

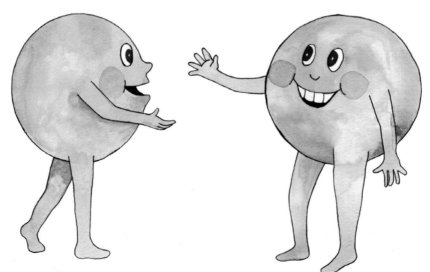

See how kind words make everyone feel better.

Secret 6: "Rest"

We must remember that in order

for us to do our best,

it is very important

that we get enough rest.

Well class, our time is up.
The bell is about to ring.
Is there anything, dear ones,
that you would like to say or sing?

36

We are so happy.

We must parade.

We are forming

the "Healthy Cell Brigade!"

We're the HEALTHY CELL BRIGADE.
What a difference these secrets have made.
We are so happy to be in the
        HEALTHY CELL BRIGADE.

Each one of you can join too.
Join the HEALTHY CELL BRIGADE.
Join the fun everyone.
Join the HEALTHY CELL BRIGADE.

The *Healthy Cell Brigade* certificate on the opposite page is designed to be signed, cut out, framed and placed in a boy's room, girl's room, kitchen or family room. The certificate fits into a standard 8x10 frame.

It is a beautiful and permanent reminder of healthy cell secrets.

Congratulations!!

You are now an official member of the
"Healthy Cell Brigade."

Sign and date certificate on the opposite page.
Cut alongside dotted lines and place in an 8X10 frame.

Healthy Cell Brigade
Membership Certificate

Awarded to

_____

Name

In recognition of completing
"Chelsea's Healthy Secrets"
you are hereby granted official
membership in
The Healthy Cell Brigade.

_____

Date

About the Author

Dr. Sherry Schiavi

Author
Nutritional Consultant
Motivational Speaker
Ordained Minister

Dr. Sherry Schiavi is Co-Founder, Nutritional Consultant and Director of Living Waters Medical Center along with her husband, Dr. Frank Schiavi. She is also the Director and Founder of Beulah Land Wellness Retreat and Trails to Success. Dr. Frank Schiavi is a Family Practitioner and Board Certified Orthopedic surgeon. A dynamic duo, he administers medical care as she educates patients on cellular nutrition and disease prevention. The results have been astounding.

Her approach is fresh, humorous and innovative; empowering children from 1-101 to develop a zest for healthy living. With the alarming rise of childhood obesity and diseases, Sherry recognized the need for a book that would educate and motivate children to make healthy lifestyle choices. She knew that it had to be fun, humorous, easy to understand and unforgettable. Thus, she created **Chelsea's Healthy Secrets**.

Sherry appears frequently at conferences, health retreats and seminars. She is known for her creative, highly motivating, humorous approach and for *"keeping it simple."*

Living Waters Medical Center is the first phase of the Schiavi's vision for a total health retreat and training center on their beautiful property in Pass Christian, Mississippi.

For Booking Information
Living Waters Medical Center
13472 Vidalia Road
Pass Christian, MS 39571
228.586.2455 *office*; 228.586.2457 *fax*

*"**Chelsea's Healthy Secrets** is an excellent, informative, and educational book. The illustrations are colorful and attractive. It is much needed in a society of unhealthy life-styles and childhood obesity. As a pediatrician, I am positive your book will be a huge success and I look forward to my patients reading **Chelsea's Healthy Secrets**."*

-Dr. William Carr, Pediatrician

*"A darling book sure to be enjoyed by children of all ages. It provides effective tools toward curbing the growing epidemic of childhood obesity and health problems. **Chelsea's Healthy Secrets** will be a key to starting a wonderful health revolution for the children of today, affecting the future of tomorrow."*

-Cynthia F. Ardoin, Former State Officer
American Cancer Society

"This is a bright, delightful and happy book. Basic solid building blocks for children's health are presented in a simple, colorful and concrete way. The appeal to children, parents and teachers are immediately obvious. In just a few pages, so much is imparted so effectively."

-Dr. Fauzia Quddus, Pediatrician

"Chelsea's Healthy Secrets is fun, energetic, and entertaining! The book is packed full of humor and written for young children to understand the importance of forming healthy life-style habits."

-Cathy Gaston, Ph.D., Head Start Director
Friends of Children of Mississippi

"Children seem to love, and more importantly grasp, the healthy cell concept. Fun and informative, this book teaches children about healthy cell secrets in a very simple and creative way."

-Hallelujah Acres
Shelby, NC

"Chelsea's Healthy Secrets is a wonderful resource tool to use as a vehicle for health success. It contains creative illustrations to make learning fun and enjoyable. "

-Regina Ginn, Director of Office of Healthy Schools
Mississippi Dept of Education

Illustrator

Elizabeth Huffmaster is a long time resident of Southern Mississippi, where she lives with her husband and two sons. She has garnered many artistic awards and achievements. Today she enjoys a productive busy career as a book illustrator and is currently under contract with several authors. Elizabeth also holds a position as an Art Therapist for the Harrison County School system in Mississippi and her work allows her to share her love of art with special needs children.

Designer/Publisher

Dionne T. Powe, owner of *Deziner Media Intl (award-winning agency) and Publishing Company*, in New Orleans, Louisiana, designed Chelsea's Healthy Secrets. *Dionne* enjoys the challenge of unique and informative projects and is delighted to have been a part of such important and vital work. You can correspond with *Deziner Media* at: dezinermedia@aol.com.